From: Aunt Betsy (Betty) 2017
and uncle Mick XO

From: Aunt Betsy (Betty) 2017

and uncle Mick XO

THE USBORNE BOOK OF
EVERYDAY WORDS

Designer and modelmaker: Jo Litchfield

Editors: Rebecca Treays, Kate Needham and Lisa Miles
Photography: Howard Allman
Modelmaker: Stefan Barnett
Managing Editor: Felicity Brooks
Managing Designer: Mary Cartwright
Photographic manipulation and design: Michael Wheatley

With thanks to Inscribe Ltd. and Eberhard Faber for providing the Fimo® modeling material

Everyday Words is a stimulating and lively wordfinder for young children. Each double page shows familiar scenes from the world around us, providing plenty of opportunity for talking and sharing.

Very young children will have fun simply spotting and naming the different objects and characters. Children who are beginning to learn to read will enjoy reading the words around the edges of the scenes. This book will also be a useful spelling guide for older children who are starting to write their own stories.

A word list at the back of the book brings together all the words in alphabetical order. This can be used to encourage children to look up words and find the right page and picture – an important skill which will prepare them for the later use of dictionaries and information books.

There are a number of hidden objects to find in every big scene. A small picture shows what to look for.

Above all, this bright and busy book will give children hours of enjoyment and a love of reading that will last.

The family

sister   brother   daughter   father   son   mother

cat   grandmother   grandfather   dog

grandson   granddaughter

The town

 Find fifteen cars

gas station

supermarket

stores

hospital

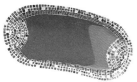

swimming pool

school

parking lot

movie theater

bridge

The street

 Find twelve birds

baker's shop

waiter

police officer

pharmacy

stroller

bus stop

6

 butcher's shop

 dog

 café

 skateboard

 firefighter

 baby buggy

 lamp post

 post office

 cat

 baker

The house

Find eight cups

door

door handle

carpet

roof

banister

attic

bedroom   study   bathroom

living room   hall   kitchen

fireplace   light switch   rug   window   stairs

9

The yard

caterpillar

Find seventeen worms

flowerpot

bee

shovel

bone

slug

ladybug

leaf

snail

ant

rake

doghouse

tree

barbecue
grill

butterfly

wheelbarrow

seeds

nest

lawnmower

11

The kitchen

Find ten tomatoes

sink

knife

washing machine

toaster

chair

saucer

table

cup

frying pan

microwave

fork

strainer

stove

spoon

dustpan

dishwasher

plate

saucepan

jug

bowl

refrigerator

Things to eat

cookie

bread

pasta

rice

flour

cereal

fruit juice

tea bag

coffee

sugar

milk

cream

butter

egg

cheese

yogurt

chicken

shrimp

sausage

bacon

fish

salami

ham

soup

pizza

salt

pepper

mustard

ketchup

honey

jelly

raisins

peanuts

water

pineapple	pear	lime	lemon	peach	apricot
cherry	banana	strawberry	raspberry	mango	grapefruit
plum	coconut	orange	watermelon	melon	grapes
apple	kiwi fruit	tomato	avocado	potato	green beans
zucchini	cabbage	onion	mushroom	carrot	eggplant
leek	broccoli	cauliflower	peas	spinach	beets
lettuce	celery	corn	cucumber	chili pepper	bell pepper

The living room

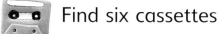 Find six cassettes

CD

coin purse

armchair

vacuum cleaner

video tape

sofa

VCR

stereo

jigsaw puzzle

television

recorder

flower

fruit bowl

tambourine

tray

cushion

piano

headphones

17

The study

 Find nine pens

desk

computer

telephone

magazine

guitar

plant

book

crayon

photograph

The bathroom

 Find three boats

soap

basin

towel

plug

toilet

bathtub

toilet paper

comb

shampoo

shower

The bedroom

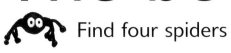

crocodile

trumpet

chest of drawers

robot

bed

teddy bear

rocket

doll

drum

spaceship

elephant

cassette

snake

alarm clock

puppet

night stand

lion

blanket

giraffe

playing cards

Around the house

toothpaste toothbrush

newspaper letter

blind curtain comforter pillow photo album

ironing board iron sewing machine vase computer mouse

potty chair sponge faucet hairbrush mirror

trash can dish soap calculator toys lamp

Transportation

ambulance

fire engine

police car

helicopter

truck

car

bulldozer

scooter

boat

kayak

trailer

airplane

hot air balloon

tractor

taxi

bicycle

bus

motorcycle

submarine

train

race car

delivery van

ski lift

sportscar

23

The farm

Find five kittens

 piglet

 pig

 goose

 bull

 cow

calf

 rooster

chick

 hen

barn

rabbit

sheep

lamb

pond

donkey

goat

farmer

turkey

gate

duckling

duck

puppy

horse

The classroom

 Find twenty crayons

 pencil sharpener

easel

pen

paper

felt-tip pen

chalk

coat hook

scissors

chalkboard

string

stool

pencil

eraser

tape

glue

blocks

paint

paintbrush

teacher

clock

notebook

ruler

The party

Find eleven apples

tape recorder

present

pirate

cowboy

doctor

chips

popcorn

balloon

ribbon

cake

chocolate

ice cream

card

ballerina

mermaid

astronaut

clown

candy

candle

straw

highchair

The campsite

suitcase

![teddy bear] Find two teddy bears

tent

camera

radio

backpack

permit

flashlight

film

money

soccer ball

umbrella

map

binoculars

kitten

ticket

Things to wear

T-shirt

jeans

overalls

dress

skirt

tights

pajamas

bathrobe

undershirt

bib

sweater

sweatshirt

cardigan

pants

apron

shirt

coat

sweat suit

32

shorts

underpants

swimsuit

swimming
trunks

bikini

tie

belt

suspenders

zipper

button

scarf

glasses

sunglasses

pin

watch

sock

glove

hat

cap

helmet

boot

tennis shoe

ballet shoe

slipper

shoe

sandal

The workshop

 Find thirteen mice

toolbox

watering can

nail

hammer

pocketknife

screwdriver

can

spider

saw

vise

key

worm

bucket

shovel

match

cardboard box

wheel

hose

rope

moth

wrench

broom

35

The park

 Find seven soccer balls

wading pool

boy

36

bird

 sandwich

tennis racket

hamburger

 kite

 baby

 hotdog

French fries

 wheelchair

 girl

 swings

seesaw

 merry-go-round

 slide

Parts of the body

head

ear

tongue

nose

mouth

teeth

eye

back

belly

belly button

arm

leg

elbow

knee

hand

foot

finger

thumb

bottom

long hair

short hair

curly hair

straight hair

Actions

sleeping

cycling

riding

smiling

laughing

crying

singing

walking

running

jumping

kicking

40

writing   painting   drawing   reading   cutting   sticking

sitting   standing   pushing   pulling

eating   drinking   bathing   kissing   waving

Shapes

 oval

 circle

 crescent

 triangle

 square

 rectangle

 star

Colors

 red

 pink

 yellow

 brown

 gray

 blue

 purple

 white

 green

 black

orange

42

Numbers

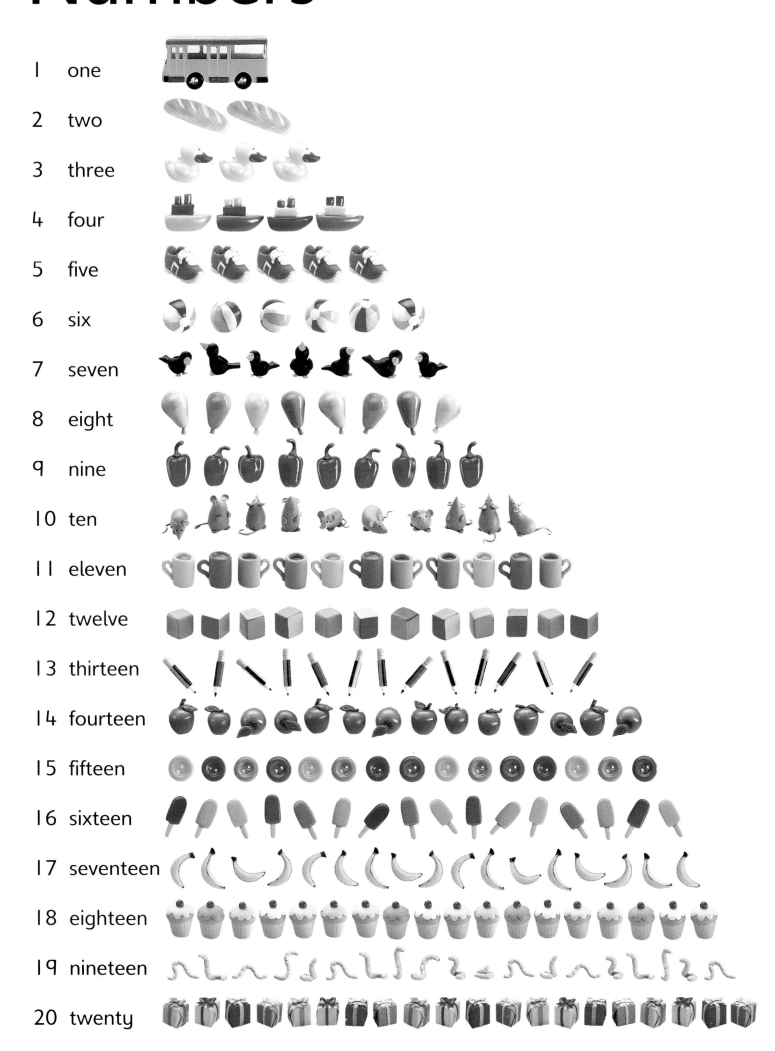

1 one

2 two

3 three

4 four

5 five

6 six

7 seven

8 eight

9 nine

10 ten

11 eleven

12 twelve

13 thirteen

14 fourteen

15 fifteen

16 sixteen

17 seventeen

18 eighteen

19 nineteen

20 twenty

43

Word list

clock, 27
clown, 29
coat, 32
coat hook, 26
coconut, 15
coffee, 14
coin purse, 16
colors, 42
comb, 19
comforter, 22
computer, 18
computer mouse, 22
cooker, 12
cookie, 14
corn, 15
cow, 24
cowboy, 28
crayon, 18
crayons, 26
cream, 14
crescent, 42
crying, 40
cucumber, 15
cup, 12
cups, 8
curly hair, 39
curtain, 22
cushion, 17
cutting, 41
cycling, 40

d daughter, 3
delivery van, 23
desk, 19
dish soap, 22
dishwasher, 12
doctor, 28
dog, 2, 7
doghouse, 11
doll, 20
donkey, 25
door, 8

door handle, 8
drawing, 41
dress, 32
drinking, 41
drum, 20
duck, 25
duckling, 25
dustpan, 12

e ear, 38
easel, 26
eating, 41
egg, 14
eggplant, 15
eight, 43
eighteen, 43
elbow, 39
elephant, 21
eleven, 43
eraser, 27
eye, 38

f family, 3
farm, 24-25
farmer, 25
father, 3
faucet, 22
felt-tip pen, 26
fifteen, 43
film (camera), 31
finger, 39
fire engine, 23
firefighter, 7
fireplace, 9
fish, 14
five, 43
flashlight, 30
flour, 14
flower, 17
flowerpot, 10
foot, 39

fork, 12
four, 43
fourteen, 43
French fries, 37
fridge, 12
fruit bowl, 17
fruit juice, 14
frying pan, 12

g gas station, 4
gate, 25
giraffe, 21
girl, 37
glasses, 33
glove, 33
glue, 27
goat, 25
goose, 24
granddaughter, 3
grandfather, 3
grandmother, 3
grandson, 3
grapefruit, 15
grapes, 15
gray, 42
green, 42
green beans, 15
guitar, 18

h hair, 39
hairbrush, 22
hall, 9
ham, 14
hamburger, 37
hammer, 34
hand, 39
hat, 33
head, 38
headphones, 17
helicopter, 23
helmet, 33
hen, 24

45

Additional models: Les Pickstock, Barry Jones, Stef Lumley and Karen Krige. With thanks to Vicki Groombridge, Nicole Irving and the Model Shop, 151 City Road, London.

First published in 1999 by Usborne Publishing Ltd, Usborne House, 83-85 Saffron Hill, London EC1N 8RT, England. www.usborne.com
Copyright © Usborne Publishing Ltd, 1999.
First published in America 1999. AE